THE MR MEN CHRISTMAS

by Roger Hargreaves

Thurman Publishing

ISBNO 85985 056 0

First published 1977 by Thurman Publishing
The Mill Trading Estate Acton Lane London NW10

For Adam and Giles, who helped a lot.

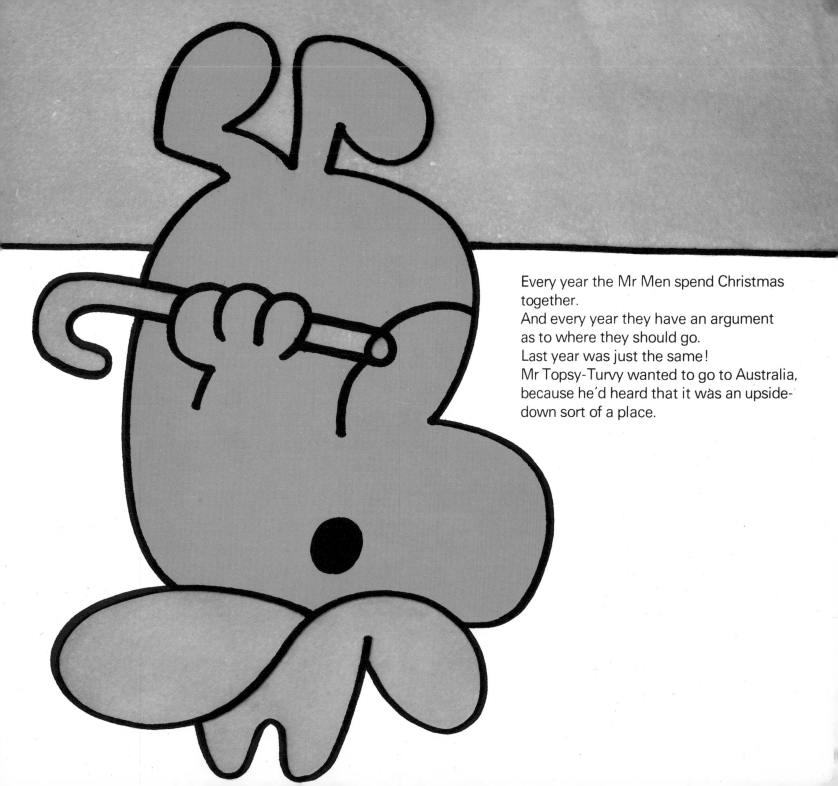

Every year the Mr Men spend Christmas together.
And every year they have an argument as to where they should go.
Last year was just the same!
Mr Topsy-Turvy wanted to go to Australia, because he'd heard that it was an upside-down sort of a place.

Mr Greedy wanted to go to France,
because he'd heard that the food there
was rather good.

Mr Muddle wanted to go to the North
Pole, because it would be nice and warm
there.

And Mr Silly wanted to go to the Moon.
How silly.

But every year
they always finished up
going to the same place.
Mr Uppity's house!

This was partly because Mr Uppity had
the only house big enough for all the
Mr Men.
And partly because Mr Uppity wouldn't
go anywhere else anyway.
So, last year, as always, on Christmas
Eve, all the Mr Men arrived at Mr Uppity's
big house in Bigtown.

Mr Silly ran all the way there.
"I was too tired to walk" he explained.

Because it was Christmas Eve all the Mr Men were very excited. Mr Bounce kept on bouncing up and down he was so excited. Mr Noisy kept saying "HAPPY CHRISTMAS" to everybody in such a loud voice it made everybody jump.

In fact, it made Mr Silly jump out of shoes!

Mr Topsy-Turvy kept on saying
"Christmas Happy" to everybody.
And Mr Greedy was seen to be licking his
lips a lot and saying "Turkey, Christmas
cake, mince pies and plum pudding" over
and over to himself.

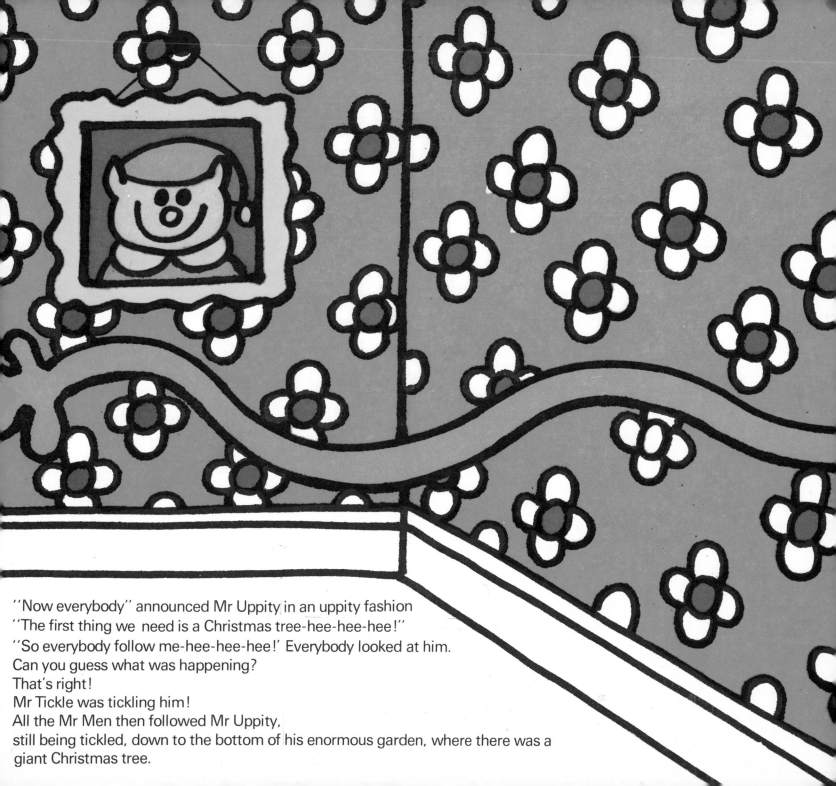

"Now everybody" announced Mr Uppity in an uppity fashion
"The first thing we need is a Christmas tree-hee-hee-hee!"
"So everybody follow me-hee-hee-hee!' Everybody looked at him.
Can you guess what was happening?
That's right!
Mr Tickle was tickling him!
All the Mr Men then followed Mr Uppity,
still being tickled, down to the bottom of his enormous garden, where there was a
giant Christmas tree.

That afternoon
they spent all afternoon
decorating it.
Mr Tickle had to put the
fairy on the top
because he was the only one w
could reach.
It looked very beautiful!

Mr Sneeze looked at it.
"ATISHOO!"
He sneezed all the decorations off.
Every single one!
So they had to do it all over again.

That Christmas Eve all the Mr Men hung all their Christmas stockings up along
Mr Uppity's enormous fireplace. Can you guess which one is Mr Topsy-Turvy's?
And which one is Mr Small's?
And which one is Mr Greedy's?
And which two are Mr Muddle's?
And can you guess who came and looked in them all before he went to bed?

Christmas morning came, and all the Mr
Men gave all the other Mr Men their presents.

Mr Daydream gave Mr Sneeze a box of handkerchiefs.

Mr Snow gave Mr Messy a comb.

Mr Happy gave Mr Lazy a cushion.

Mr Impossible gave Mr Chatterbox a dictionary so that he could say even more words than he could already.

Mr Mean gave Mr Forgetful a lump of coal. And Mr Forgetful forgot to say thank you. But he did remember to give Mr Small a new hat. But did he remember to make sure it was the right size?

No!

And Mr Silly gave Mr Uppity a very special present.
A Nonsenseland teapot!

After that, they all went into
Mr Uppity's dining room to eat
Turkey, Christmas cake,
mince pies and
plum pudding!
And beside everybody's
plate was a
Christmas cracker.
Mr Topsy-Turvy and
Mr Happy pulled one of
the crackers.

BANG!

Poor Mr Jelly nearly jumped out of his skin.
And hid under the table.

All the Christmas crackers had paper hats
inside them, and all the Mr Men put them
on and tucked into their Christmas dinner.
Mr Greedy had twenty slices of turkey.
Then Christmas cake.
Thirty slices !
Then mince pies.
Forty pies !
Then plum pudding !

One minute it was there, the next minute
it wasn't.
"Delicious" murmured Mr Greedy
wiping away a crumb.

That afternoon it snowed.
Mr Fussy looked out of the window.
"Oh what a terrible mess all that snow's making" he said, and rushed outside to clear it all up.
Which of course he couldn't!

Mr Tickle discovered that his
extraordinarily long arms were very
useful for throwing snowballs.
Especially as he was sitting comfortably
inside!

Mr Bump walked into a tree, and all the
snow fell on top of him and turned him
into a snowman!

Mr Bounce fell over, and rolled down a
hill in the snow and became a snowball!

And you should have seen Mr Topsy- Turvy on a toboggan!

And guess who sang the loudest when
they sang Christmas carols that evening?
After that, Mr Muddle thought that he'd
like to say ''Happy Christmas'' to
everybody.
He opened his mouth.
All the Mr Men looked at him.

"Happy Birthday" he said.
Oh Mr Muddle.
Happy Christmas!

PRINTED IN ENGl